"HELLO READING books are a perfect introduction to reading. Brief sentences full of word repetition and full-color pictures stress visual clues to help a child take the first important steps toward reading. Mastering these story books will build children's reading confidence and give them the enthusiasm to stand on their own in the world of words."

—Bee Cullinan
Past President of the International Reading
Association, Professor in New York University's
Early Childhood and Elementary Education Program

"Readers aren't born, they're made. Desire is planted—planted by parents who work at it."

—Jim Trelease
author of *The Read Aloud Handbook*

"When I was a classroom reading teacher, I recognized the importance of good stories in making children understand that reading is more than just recognizing words. I saw that children who have ready access to story books get excited about reading. They also make noticeably greater gains in reading comprehension. The development of the HELLO READING stories grows out of this experience."

—Harriet Ziefert
M.A.T., New York University School of Education
Author, Language Arts Module,
Scholastic Early Childhood Program

VIKING KESTREL
Viking Penguin Inc., 40 West 23rd Street,
New York, New York 10010, U.S.A.
Penguin Books Ltd., Harmondsworth, Middlesex, England
Penguin Books Australia Ltd., Ringwood, Victoria, Australia
Penguin Books Canada Limited, 2801 John St., Markham, Ontario, Canada
Penguin Books (N.Z.) Ltd., 182–190 Wairau Rd., Auckland 10, New Zealand

First published in 1987
3   5   7   9   10   8   6   4   2
Published simultaneously in Canada
Text copyright © Harriet Ziefert, 1987
Illustrations copyright © Catherine Siracusa, 1987

ISBN 0-670-81719-8 Library of Congress Catalog Card No: 86-40481
Printed in Singapore for Harriet Ziefert, Inc.

Mike and Tony:
Best Friends

Harriet Ziefert
Pictures by Catherine Siracusa

VIKING KESTREL

Mike and Tony
were buddies.

They walked
to school together.

They ate lunch together.

Mike picked Tony
for his team.

And Tony picked Mike.

After school
they played ball...

and tag...

and leapfrog.

Sometimes they rode bikes.

And sometimes they did
nothing much at all.

Every Friday night Mike and Tony had a sleep-over.

They took turns
getting cookies.

They took turns calling
their friends on the phone.

One Friday night
Mike and Tony had
a pillow fight.

It was a small pillow
fight that grew…

and grew...

and grew!

Mike and Tony threw
down their pillows.

They grabbed each other
and wrestled.

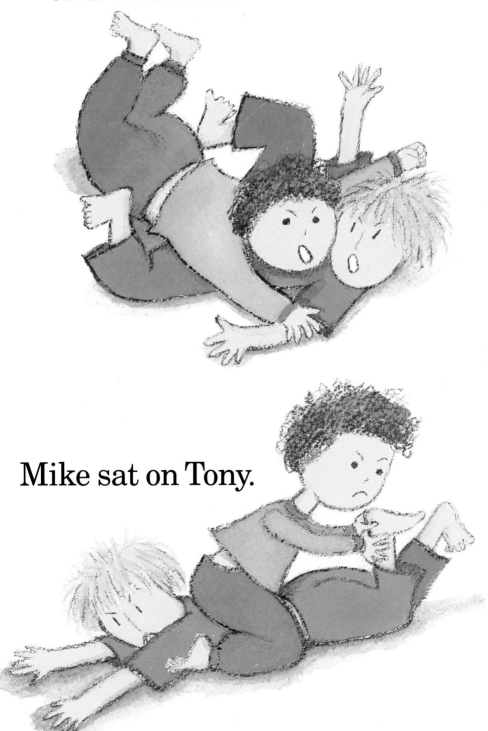

Mike sat on Tony.

And Tony sat on Mike.
He yelled, "I win!"

Mike shouted, "You did not! You cheat!"

Mike took his sleeping bag
and ran out the door.

Tony called his mother.
"Mike ran away!"

"Let's go find him,"
said Tony's mother.

Mike was still mad.
He yelled, "You didn't win!"

Tony said, "Okay! Okay!
I didn't win. Nobody did."

Mike and Tony
were buddies again.